SMALL TOWN EVIL 2

By Ken Berglund

W0082202

Text Copyright © 2014

Kenneth M. Berglund

All Rights Reserved

This book is protected under international copyright law and is licensed for your personal use only. No part of this publication may be copied, reproduced in any format by an means, electronic or otherwise, without prior consent from the copyright owner.

TABLE OF CONTENTS

"Conscience is no more than the dead speaking to us."

- Jim Carroll

PART ONE – MURDER IN TEXAS...SCARS IN CALIFORNIA

CHAPTER 1

Six-year-old Max Wilkins stood at the corner of his street, waiting for the bus, as he usually did every morning. The morning ritual was always the same. His father, Christopher Wilkins, would come into his room at 6:15am, cell phone in hand, and play the theme song for "Angry Birds." Once Max heard the music, he would jump from his bed right away. A simple alarm clock wouldn't work. It had to be a video game.

Then it was breakfast time. A small box of Corn Pops, Froot Loops, or Frosted Flakes would usually do the trick, followed by a mug of hot chocolate.

"Daddy, did you sign my folder?" he asked his father. Chris knew he had to sign that school folder every day or else his son would get a red mark. A red mark was not good.

"Yeah, I signed it last night," he said, holding his morning cup of coffee and watching the morning news. There was yet another crisis in Washington, D.C.

"Is my lunch in my backpack? We need to go to the bus stop," Max said to his father.

"I just want to see this news story really quick. I'll meet up with you there," Chris said.

"Fine," Max said, disappointed that his father was so distracted. He picked up his Spongebob Squarepants backpack and walked out the door.

• • • • •

The Stranger, a tall, slender man who wore a long leather coat and a rather snappy black fedora hat, took immediate notice that Max was alone on the street corner and approached him. He knew that other kids would soon arrive, but Max was early today.

"Is this the spot where we wait for the bus?" The Stranger asked Max.

"It's a school bus, not a regular bus," Max answered.

"Of course it is. Silly me," The Stranger said and laughed, exposing a mouth of yellow, rotting teeth.

"Yuck! What's wrong with your teeth?"

"I'm sorry, did that scare you? I guess I shouldn't have smiled," The Stranger answered. "I'm actually on my way to see the dentist, and I thought I could catch a ride on this bus."

"You can't go to the dentist on the school bus, silly!"

"You're right. I don't know what I was thinking," The Stranger answered. He reached into his pocket, pulling out a piece of paper. "You know, I have this map here. It shows where all the bus stations are. Do you think you can tell me where this place is?" He placed the paper in front of Max's face. It looked like a child's drawing, with random scribbles covering the page.

"I can't really read…" Max began but was cut off when The Stranger covered his face with a cloth. The chloroform took effect immediately. The Stranger had taken Max in less than two minutes. His father arrived at the empty street corner about a minute later. Max was gone.

CHAPTER 2

Jack Taylor, now at age 47, had not had a successful date in the past five years. It was as though he had been cursed with a spell that made him toxic to the female population. The scars on his face, which he never spoke of, didn't particularly help him in the looks department either. When he spoke of his ex-wife, Alice, and his 13-year-old daughter, Jennifer, it was often met with "What? YOU were married before?" As he got out of his compact little Honda FIT, outside the trendy Mexican restaurant Catalina Joe's, he could see his date waiting outside. Jack was dressed in beige slacks and a black t-shirt, and carried a bouquet of flowers, but when his date caught a glimpse of him, he immediately knew this was unlikely to go well.

"Are you Judy?" he asked. She was attractive, though nothing to write home about. She looked about 50, but she tried to hide her age as much as possible. Her dyed blonde hair, breast implants, and her *Def Leppard PYROMANIA Tour* t-shirt pretty much told him all he needed to know. She was a party chick, but her party went on 25 years too long.

"Yeah, that's me," she answered.

"It's only 5:20. You're ten minutes early," he said to her, but then wondered why that was even important.

"A friend of mine drove me here. She just dropped me off a few minutes ago. Are those for me?" She asked, eyeing the flowers.

"Oh…yes they are," Jack answered, almost forgetting he was still holding them. He handed them over and she accepted them unenthusiastically.

"Thanks. So you like this restaurant, huh?" she asked.

"Well, since I knew from your profile that you loved Mexican food, I thought this would be a great place for us to meet for dinner. I've been here several times. Best chips and salsa I've ever had."

"Sounds good, then. Let's see if it lives up to your high praise," Judy said.

• • • • •

Amanda was gone. It was only Jennifer now, and that's how it had been for years. Now, at 13 years old, she had grown into a very attractive young woman. Though she had seen countless psychiatrists and paranormal psychics, there came a point when they all agreed that this ghost that had haunted her and her father was no longer a threat. She had moved on, they claimed, to the other world. Her business completed. Ghosts, they explained, don't like to remain in the world of the living if they don't have a reason for it. With Amanda's murder solved and her killer dead, she simply had no reason to stay any longer.

Yet, as Jennifer sat on her father's sofa that Saturday night, waiting for an update on his latest date (which she had begged him to go on), she felt a rather uneasy feeling tingling through her body. Breaking into her favorite TV show, which was yet another variation on "American Idol," the local insipid news reporter diverted her attention.

"ANOTHER CHILD ABDUCTION IN CENTRAL TEXAS, AND POLICE FEAR THIS COULD BE ANOTHER VICTIM OF ONE OF THE WORST SERIAL KILLERS IN TEXAS HISTORY."

It didn't matter that Jennifer and her father lived in California. When it's a serial killer who targets children, the entire country knows about it. The Stranger was particularly brutal, murdering every child he took, never sparing a single one, and always cutting out their hearts before dumping their bodies in a field or an isolated farm road (of which there were so many in Texas.) He typically kept his victims for three days, and poor Max Wilkins' time was running out.

"Fucking Texas," Jennifer said to herself, and then again she felt something move within her body. This time it was more than a tingling sensation. She looked at her hand and watched as the veins began to bounce, almost as if in some sort of dance.

"What the hell is happening to me?" she asked to no one as the feeling in her body subsided. Behind her, in the kitchen, a solitary glass that had been left in the sink, shattered to pieces.

· · · · ·

"So…." Jack began.

"So…" Judy continued.

Well, this is going nowhere fast.

"So tell me a little more about yourself? Any hobbies? What do you like to do?" Jack asked.

"I'm a pretty boring person, actually. I don't have many hobbies. I mostly just spend my free time watching TV," Judy responded.

"You need to get out more."

"I do. I go out plenty. You know, Whitesnake is coming to town next month. That'll be an awesome show," Judy said, showing a look of excitement that had clearly been lacking up to this point.

Time just froze for you in 1987, didn't it?

"Really? The singer, though, isn't he around 70 years old by now?"

"No, he's 62," Judy answered, acting as though the question offended her. "Still hot, though."

"Okay, okay, 62. My fault."

"What about you? What's your story? How about those scars on your face? Looks like you got in a brawl with someone that didn't turn out so well," Judy inquired.

A brawl would have been preferable. Unfortunately, no, it just happened to be a sadistic piece of shit serial-killer pedophile that was seconds away from chopping my God damned head off.

"Bar fight," Jack said, preferring not to relive that moment in time. At least not with *this* particular woman.

"Must have been a hell of a bar fight."

"Yeah. The asshole brought a straight razor. Couldn't face me man-to-man without a weapon," Jack said.

"I hope you at least fucked him up as much as he did you."

Yeah, police were picking up pieces of his brain for hours after his sister blew his miserable fucking head off.

"Yeah. I'd say he got the worst of it," Jack said.

"So where do you work?" Judy asked after a long pause.

"Well, I used to be an engineer, but I gave that up when I had to take care of my daughter full time. Now I just do a lot of temp jobs. Enough to pay the bills."

"You have a daughter?"

There it is again. Is it really that impossible to imagine me having a daughter? I'm 47 years old, I haven't ALWAYS been the pathetic guy I am now. You try dealing with the post-traumatic stress that I've been dealing with and see how it affects you.

"Yes. She's thirteen. The jewel of my life."

"Awww, that's really sweet," Judy said. "So her mother doesn't share in any of the parental responsibilities?"

"No…she's had some…well, I guess the best way to say it would be…*issues.* She's had some issues."

Much to both of their delight, the waitress appeared with their food, carrying two enormous plates.

"Shrimp fajitas?" she asked.

"Mine," Judy answered.

"And you had the chicken burrito," the waitress continued and set the plate down. "Be careful. The plates are hot."

Jack noticed immediately that something was wrong with his order. Rather than the typical *green* sauce that is poured over the chicken burritos, this one had *red* sauce. Had he not been to this restaurant so many times before, he would have neither noticed nor cared.

"Excuse me, but I think this is wrong," Jack said to the waitress. "I don't think this is chicken. The sauce isn't green, it's red. I think you brought me a steak burrito by mistake."

Judy looked down at the table as if to say *I wish I was anywhere but here.*

"All the burritos have red sauce. We don't use green sauce anymore," the waitress explained. Jack wasn't hearing it. He quickly cut into the burrito like a madman to prove his point.

"You see! That's steak," he proudly exclaimed, and the waitress quickly glanced at it.

"It's chicken. The meat is just a little dark, but it's chicken, I assure you."

"Come on, I know steak when I see it. Just admit you got the order wrong. I'd like a new one. One that actually has chicken inside it," Jack demanded.

"OK, fine," the waitress said reluctantly, picking up the plate and quickly walking away. Jack then looked at Judy, who was now shooting daggers at him with her eyes.

"Are you usually this embarassing when you go out in public?" she asked him.

"I've ordered the chicken burrito at least a dozen times, and it's never looked like that. It's not my fault they got the order wrong. If you don't speak up for yourself then people will walk all over you."

"OK, OK, I just want to eat."

· · · · ·

Jennifer stared at the shattered glass in the sink and thought of every possible scenario that may have caused it.

Thermal shock. Yes, that must be it! Except...from what? The glass was dry.

"Okay, let's not get paranoid," she said to herself, and suddenly her cell phone rang to the tune of Katy Perry's latest insufferable hit song.

UNKNOWN CALLER the iPhone read, but unlike her father, who would never answer such a call, Jennifer was just so happy to have her own iPhone that she answered *everything.*

"Hello?" she asked and was answered by silence on the other end. "You got five seconds to answer, or I'm hanging up."

"I'm sorry," a voice faintly said. It sounded like that of a child. A boy. "I'm looking for someone, and I was given this number."

"Who are you looking for?" Jennifer asked.

"I'm looking for...Amanda."

· · · · ·

"Everything okay now?" the waitress asked Jack after handing him a new plate with a new, freshly cooked chicken burrito.

"Yes, everything is fine. Thank you, and I'm sorry if I upset you earlier," Jack replied.

"Don't worry about it," the waitress told him, but he could tell from the look on her face that she hated her job, and particularly, *customers like him.*

He began to cut into his food but stopped abruptly, focusing rather sharply on the melted cheese poured on top. Something looked...*wrong.*

"This looks like spit," he said. "These fucking guys spit on my food, just because I returned it."

Judy, who now was only mere seconds from walking out, looked at him.

"What in the FUCK is wrong with you, guy?" she asked him, quite simply.

"Look at it yourself!"

She quickly glanced over, "I don't see a God damn thing, and I am about THIS close to walking out," she said, revealing her thumb and index finger *extremely* close together.

"Excuse me. Miss!" Jack shouted to the waitress, who conveniently ignored him.

"That's it. I'm gone. You have officially made this the worst date of my entire life," Judy said and stood up.

"Let's just go somewhere else. I promise you I'm not usually like this," Jack tried to explain.

"I don't give a fuck what you're usually like. I'm done. Just give that poor girl the tip she deserves for having to deal with assholes like you all day."

Jack quickly fumbled through his wallet to grab some loose bills, tossing them down on the table along with...quite unexpectedly...a packaged condom, which landed directly on top of his food.

"UGH," was all Judy could make out.

"I'm sorry," Jack exclaimed, clearly embarassed. He had definitely seen better days.

"You really thought the night was going to go that way? You think I'm that loose?"

"Really, I am truly sorry."

"Go fuck yourself," was the last thing she said to him.

CHAPTER 3

When Jack arrived home that night he was surprised to see that his daughter had waited up for him. Jennifer certainly wouldn't have had it any other way. She loved her father, and in the years that had passed, their bond had only grown stronger. As much as she hated the idea of having a stepmother, she *wanted* him to find love again. It pained her to see the pathetic loser he was slowly evolving into.

"So…spill the beans," she said with a smile.

"You don't want to know," he said.

"Of course I do!"

"No, you don't. Trust me. You don't."

"It couldn't have been that bad, could it?" Jennifer asked.

"About as bad as it could possibly be. I'm officially the biggest asshole on the planet. I'm pretty sure once news of this date gets out, no woman will go within fifty feet of me."

"That bad, huh?"

"Yeah. So what about you? How was your night?" Jack asked her.

"Pretty normal except for a weird phone call I received. It was an unknown caller, and I didn't get the number, but there was something really weird about it," Jennifer said, and Jack began to look concerned.

"Really? Did they say anything?"

"It was a little boy, and it was a wrong number, but the *name* he asked for…" Jennifer began.

No…don't say the name I think you're going to say.

"Amanda," Jennifer finished. "I know that name meant something to me when I was just little. My whole body just felt weird when I heard him say it."

"Like you said, it was probably just a wrong number. I wouldn't worry about it much," Jack said to her and hoped that a wrong number was *all* it was. Somewhere, though, in the back of his mind, he knew that this was likely just the beginning.

"Are you ever going to tell me exactly what happened? With Amanda? The scars on your face?" she asked.

"I will. Someday. I promise. Let's just get some sleep now."

CHAPTER 4

Jennifer opened her eyes to the blue glow of her alarm clock, which read **3:33a.m.** Her room was unusually quiet. No sounds of crickets or car alarms blaring outside, as was almost a nightly occurrence in their apartment. She looked around her room, glancing at her Katy Perry and Lady Gaga posters. She even looked at the gap in her wall where was once a Justin Bieber poster that had been rather abruptly torn down. Sitting at the foot of her bed, however, was something that hadn't been there before. A Disney Princess Tea Set.

"What the hell?" she said to herself.

"Hello, Jennifer. What will it be? Coffee, tea, or juice?" a voice asked out from the darkness.

"Who is that?" Jennifer asked.

"You don't remember me?" the voice asked back, and Jennifer could make out a shape beginning to emerge from her closet. She could see it was just a young girl, about 8 years old, with long blonde hair, but she could not see her face clearly, but she *knew* who it was.

"Who or what the fuck are you?" Jennifer asked, angrily.

"My, my, my. You've really developed a potty mouth over the years, haven't you? Don't you know it's not very classy for a girl to swear?"

"Just tell me what the fuck you want…Amanda."

"There you go. I knew you'd remember me," Amanda said.

"Please, just go away!" Jennifer shouted.

"Oh, come on, Jen. Can't it be like it was? We can play Princess again like we used to," Amanda said.

"I'm not eight years old anymore! I've outgrown that!" Jennifer shouted angrily.

"Right. I guess you have, haven't you? I guess we'll just have to talk like grown ups now," Amanda said.

"I don't want to talk to you. You're not real. You're just a figment of my imagination."

"I'm much more than that, Jennifer. I'm your power. A power you have not fully realized. Remember the glass? That was me," Amanda explained.

"Why are you back?" Jennifer asked.

"There's a man in Texas doing some very, very bad things. Evil things. He must be stopped," Amanda replied.

"Why do you care about that? What, did he kill you or something? You want revenge?" Jennifer asked her, annoyed.

"LOOK AT ME!" Amanda shouted and jumped on the bed next to Jennifer. Her face was skeletal and rotted, her blonde hair the only trace of the beautiful girl she once was. "YOU ARE GOING TO DO THIS!"

Jennifer screamed as her father opened the door and turned on the light.

"Are you alright, baby?" he asked. She opened her eyes. Amanda and the tea set had disappeared, as she knew they would. She began to cry.

"No," she answered. "I'm not."

CHAPTER 5

At 62 years of age, Lawrence Phillips was just as spry as anyone in The Agency that was half his age. Not that it mattered. His days were numbered, and at this point his memoirs had all but written themselves, with maybe one more chapter left. As he walked into the kitchen for breakfast, he looked as though he had just stepped out of *GQ Magazine.* His gray hair nicely slicked back, the gray goatee neatly trimmed, and not a single crease in his fine Italian suit. His wife, who stood by the stove, barely acknowledged his presence.

"You want scrambled eggs?" she said into the air, never looking at him.

"Sure," he answered, then proceeded to make himself a cup of coffee and sit at the table. His wife, Gretchen, certainly hadn't kept up her appearance the way her husband had. She had *gone to pot,* as Lawrence once heard his own father say about his mother.

"Your mother has pretty much *gone to pot!*" his father told him, which, roughly translated, meant *Your mother disgusts me now, and the reason you never hear any noises coming from our bedroom anymore is because we stopped fucking years ago.*

While his wife cooked his eggs, he opened a manila envelope the size of a piece of paper. Inside the envelope was a single, black and white photo of Jennifer Taylor. It was something she had clearly not posed for. On the back of the photo was a handwritten note which read:

PROBABILITY 75%

· · · · ·

Approximately 1400 miles away, The Stranger kept a close eye on five-year-old Gabriela Johnson as she attended her fourth ballet lesson at the Galaxy Dance Studio in Austin, Texas. Unlike Max, the last poor, unfortunate soul to cross his eye, this wasn't to be a spur-of-the-moment abduction. The taking of Max was rather sloppy in his view, and now, with more and more parents guarding their children like a hawk, he knew it was something he could not easily repeat.

The Stranger was an avid Facebook junkie. Though he considered himself a friend to no-one, people still wanted to be friends with *him.* At least a dozen former high-school classmates had friended him on the social network. It didn't matter that he never spoke to these people in high school. It only mattered that they went to the *same* high school. One such "friend" was Candace Graves, who had a rather boast-worthy following of 1,036 "friends." It was from Miss Popularity herself, Candace, that little Gabriela was discovered.

The Stranger had only to look at the *friends* of Candace, and the friends of *their* friends until he felt the connection was far too distant to ever be traced. While many people blocked any trace of personal information to the outside world, others seemed to expose it with a sense of pride. Rachel Johnson was one such person. Her entire life was an open book.

"Gabby's first ballet lesson at Galaxy Dance studio!" One such post read, accompanied with a picture of little Gabriela in her tutu. *"First lesson is free, next five are big $$$$$"*

Rachel was astonishingly dense, going as far as revealing that she would be having her nails done in the salon two shops over from the dance studio at the same time. She loved her daughter, but she loved herself more. Watching the ballet lessons were a bore, so it made sense for her to treat herself at every given opportunity. The Stranger knew there would be a window of opportunity when Gabriela had to walk over to meet her mother.

"Gabby!" he shouted at her when he saw her exit the studio. She stopped and looked at him, an innocent smile on her face. She thought if he knew her name, he must be okay.

"Who are you?" she asked.

"Your mom wanted me to give you some Little Mermaid dolls. They're over here in the car."

"Really?"

"Yeah. Little Mermaid and Cinderella. Those are your favorites, right? I bought the wrong ones for my daughter. I was supposed to get Sleeping Beauty."

"I like Sleeping Beauty," she said, still smiling.

"Who doesn't? But you know, I can't return these, and I don't want to just throw them away. Just come take a look. If you don't like them, you don't have to take them," he reassured her.

"OK," she said and walked with him. It was the last time she was ever seen.

• • • • •

Lawrence Phillips watched as Jack Taylor dropped his daughter off outside West Middle School. Jennifer was nearing the end of her 8th grade year and soon to enter high school. As Jack drove off, he slowly and carefully followed behind. He didn't expect Jack would notice anyway. Why would he? Why would anyone *want* to follow him? He led a rather mundane life, and his current job didn't offer much in the way of satisfaction. Jack pulled into the parking lot of North Harbor Medical Center, where he currently worked as a part-time registrar.

Mr. Phillips had no intention of observing Jack at work. His time was far more valuable to him. Rather, once Jack had exited his little Honda FIT, he very quickly walked over to it and inserted a tracking device on the underside of the car.

CHAPTER 6

There was blood. A lot of blood. Like a running faucet, it spilled onto the pristine white floor of the cold emergency room. A young man no more than nineteen stumbled into the waiting room, a machete firmly lodged into his skull. Remarkably, he was alive and coherent, the blade having missed his brain by mere inches. His face, however, was not so lucky. It had been split in two. The blade had cut through his face in a diagonal pattern, through his left eye, nose, and lips. Whoever had put this machete into this man's face had done so with such force that he clearly had no intention of simply injuring him. He wanted this young man dead. Yet the man was strong and held on. He wasn't ready to die. Instead, like many others on the verge of death, he found himself at the mercy of the staff of North Harbor Medical Center.

"Puuuuhlllleeezzzeee, hellllp me," he managed the mumble through his blood-soaked lips. The triage nurse, having never seen such a grisly sight in all her seven years of nursing, sprang from her seat at the front desk and called for immediate assistance.

I don't think I'll be getting his insurance information anytime soon. The poor bastard.

The only ER doctors on staff at this time in the evening had to temporarily abandon their current patients (which wasn't much of a problem, as this evening was a typical one in the emergency room, with its usual assortment of headaches, nausea, and toothaches) and spring to the waiting room. Dr. Weston, an attractive man in his early 40's, with streaks of gray running through his brown hair, had seen it all, yet his reaction upon seeing this young man wasn't much different from anyone else.

"Holy shit…okay let's prep this guy for the OR, stat!" he shouted to the nurse, who then looked at Jack.

"We need labels and armbands for this patient, ASAP. Just use *John Doe* for now," she said, and with that the man was put onto a stretcher and rushed away, leaving the blood-soaked waiting room looking like something you might see in a third-world hospital in the midst of a civil war.

· · · · ·

"Someone FUCK ME, please!" a woman in a red gown shouted out as she walked through the hallway, escorted by a police officer. While most of the patients wore the typical blue gowns, the patients wearing the red gowns were the "special" ones. The drunks. The drug addicts. The homicidal and the suicidal, and the just plain ol' fucked up patients. As Jack passed the woman in the hallway, she lifted her gown up to reveal her naked body underneath. He looked briefly, noticing she had a rather large pot-belly and sagging breasts, with pubic hair that probably hadn't been trimmed in decades.

"Wooohooo!" she shouted, but Jack ignored her and walked on, retreating to "The Box." "The Box" was what the Admissions Department endearingly referred to when talking about their cramped office space. On this particular morning, Jack was working with Susan Partridge. She was an older woman, about 55. She looked worn, haggard, and burned out. Years working in the ER had given her permanent dark circles under her eyes, and the long periods of sitting, crouched over a computer, had not been kind to her body. She was at least eighty five pounds overweight, her stomach hanging over her belt like a sack of potatoes.

"Looks like you have a fan out there," she said to him, smiling. "She yer type?" Susan loved to play this game with the men in the ER. She would love to look at the female patients, point them out to the men, and then....*she yer type?* Susan had been single for at least 20 years, and her desperation at this point was painfully obvious. Unless they were gay (and some were), she flirted with every single man she worked with.

"Not really, no," Jack replied. "I don't go for the crazy ones."

"Yeah, I know. You like them petite girls," Susan said. She knew Jack was divorced, and she tried to flirt at every opportunity.

"So what's the story on the guy with the machete to his face? You hear anything?"

"Oh, yeah. I heard he's stable now. You should go back in there and get 'em registered," Susan told him.

"I saw a cop in his room about an hour ago. What's up with that?"

"You didn't hear?" Susan asked, a look of excitement rushing to her face. "That guy was trying to rob a liquor store. Turns out, the owner had a machete under his counter and whacked the guy with it before the guy knew what's what. I guess that guy won't be robbing no more liquor stores now."

"Holy shit."

· · · · ·

Jack entered the Machete Man's room, his clipboard in hand, hoping to get some information from him. Any information. If there was one thing the management at the hospital hated, it was an anonymous patient. Even if a patient was slightly coherent, every attempt needed to be made to at least get their social security number. From that, they can be tracked down. The worst thing a registrar could possibly do is let a patient leave without getting any information, as this would result in *non payment.*

"Hello. My name is Jack. I'm with Admissions and Registrations. If possible, I just need to ask you a few quick questions," he said to the Machete Man. The man looked in no shape to do anything. His face was covered in bandages, looking like a mummy. Jack felt guilty having to disturb him, but this was the job, like it or not.

"Ugggghhhhrruuummm," the man mumbled.

"I'm very sorry I have to ask you these questions. We just want to get you into our system so the doctors can create a medical record for you," Jack told him, which wasn't entirely true. The man's medical record was already created under *John Doe.* He only said this to make it seem like his work was more urgent than it really was. Basically, it was all about *the money*.

I need your name and your fucking social security number so the hospital can get its fucking money. I hope you realize how expensive it's going to be to treat you. This is the U S of freaking A, and we don't like charity cases here.

The man looked at Jack through his one working eye, and he motioned for him to get closer. Jack got closer to him, hovering over him.

"I just need your name and your social security number, if you know it," Jack asked him. Again, the man motioned for him to get closer. Jack leaned over him, his ear almost directly next to the man's mouth.

"Do you see her?" the man asked him in a whisper.

"Excuse me?"

"Your girl," he said, almost a croak.

"I don't understand."

"Amanda," he whispered. "She's here, and she's not alone."

"I'm sorry. What did you just say to me? I don't know anyone by that name." Jack told him, but hearing that name from a complete stranger sent cold shivers down his back.

"Room 17," he said, and was gone. The ER doctors would officially pronounce him dead fifteen minutes later.

• • • • •

This is a shit job. This is a shit job. This is a shit job. I hate this fucking job. God, how I hate it.

As he walked into his supervisor's office for his performance review, all Jack could think about was that he would rather be someplace else. After a series of meaningless temp jobs, he accepted a permanent, part-time job as an Admissions Registrar for North Harbor Medical Center. He had been working in the Emergency Room, checking in patients, asking for insurance payments, and collecting money whenever possible. It was an easy job, and it paid well, but working amongst college students and older washouts, it seemed beneath him. Still, it kept him busy and thinking about something other than the events of five years ago.

Marli Johnson, a rotund little woman who took her position as Patient Access Director a little too seriously, decorated her office with candles and incense. The glow of the computer monitor reflecting off her glasses made her all the more creepy. The smell of the incense was a little overpowering to Jack, and he hoped (and prayed) this review would be over quick.

"Please, have a seat," she told him, motioning toward the chair in front of her. "Forgive the lighting, my eyes are sensitive."

"No problem," Jack said. A lie, for certain. He watched as she adjusted herself in her chair, noticing particles of food falling from her blouse. She held a letter opener in her hand, with the intention of reading her mail at the same time as giving Jack his performance evaluation. The glare on the letter opener shined into Jack's eyes and looked like a knife. He could then feel the scars on his face throb. Another reminder of how he nearly lost his life to a psychopath.

"How are things going at home?" she asked him.

Fuck, she just has to go there.

"We take each day as it comes. Some days are better than others," he answered.

"You know, if you ever need anyone to talk to, the management team is always here to help. We're a tight rockin' ship here. You know that, right?"

"Yeah," Jack replied under a forced laugh.

"So, anyway, you're here for your review. I don't want to hold you up too long, so let's get on with it," Marli said and shuffled some paperwork in front of her. "I've been looking over your QA scores, and they're all quite good. You know your job well, and the patients seem to like you. You're on time, you help your co-workers when required. I can definitely see you in a lead position at this company. There's just one thing that's holding you back."

Here it comes. This is where she talks about the money.

"Collections?" he asked, though he already knew that was it.

"That's right. Collections. I've been looking at your collections over the past few months, and you only hit your goal once. You know that part of your job requirements for this position are to collect co-pays from patients. They know they owe the money, it's just a matter of asking them."

"That's easier said than done. Most of the patients I talk to are either uninsured, or they have Medicaid or Medicare," Jack explained.

"Then you need to try harder with those uninsured patients. You have to try to get something from them. Anything. Even a dollar is better than nothing. If they say they don't have anything, tell them to ask a friend or family member. Maybe they have a car they can sell."

Am I really having this conversation? She wants me to tell these uninsured, sick patients to sell off all their belongings? To sell their car, for fuck sake?

"Most of these people have nothing," Jack said.

"That's what they tell you, but it's not true. Look, Jack. The hospital doesn't run a charity. We're a business, like any other. Payment is expected after a patient receives service. Let's say you owned a hamburger stand. Would you give all your hamburgers away for free just because the customer can't afford it?"

No, but then again, I wouldn't charge $600 for a freakin' hamburger, either.

"No, of course not," he answered.

"You're a good employee, Jack. However, you need to get over this fear, or guilt, or whatever it is, and start collecting. This is considered a verbal warning. If you continually fail to meet your collection goals, the next step will be written, and finally termination. I don't want to lose you, but the policy is clear."

How about you try telling a patient that his Tylenol and band aid are going to cost him $300?

"I understand," Jack said, calmly. On the inside, he felt like screaming. He knew she was hoping for some reaction from him, but he didn't want to give her the satisfaction. She loved the power of her position, and if he showed any sign of breaking, it would only empower her more.

"Now, this is what we have in mind for you. There's a position that just opened up in Labor and Delivery. It's the N12 shift, 6pm to 6am."

"The graveyard shift," Jack continued.

"Well, I don't like to call it that. Sounds too morbid for me. We just call it the N12 shift around here. I know you've done nights a few times, right?"

"Only once," he answered. "I prefer to be at home with my daughter as much as possible."

"I understand that, but we think this might be a good fit for you, and it's definitely a good chance to increase your collections. You'll just be dealing with women having babies. No homeless people. No drunks. No drug addicts. A lot of the patients you'll come into contact with are already pre-scheduled and they already know how much they owe," Marli explained.

"I'm not so sure I can get used to those hours," Jack said, and he meant it. He wasn't a young man anymore. The N12 shift was a real test of endurance. He had only worked the shift one time before, but that was enough for him. The hospital had been so swamped with patients, all of them thinking they had contracted the flu, that every employee was required to work at least one N12 shift. He remembered as the time approached 2 and 3am, he began to hear a ringing in his ears, and became quite light-headed.

"Everyone says that," Marli told him, though Jack doubted that she herself had ever worked the shift. Certainly not in the ER. "You'll also get a pay differential for those hours. It's about a dollar more per hour."

The pay increase appealed to him, but it wasn't enough for what he would have to give in return.

"And if I don't want the position?"

"We have some new people coming in to work in the ER. This is the only position we have for you. L&D is perfect for someone like you. An *older* gentleman. Research has shown that expectant mothers react more positively to older staff. They feel they are better trained and more professional," Marli told him.

Basically, take this position or fuck off and die.

"Ok," Jack said. "I quit."

CHAPTER 7

When Jennifer walked through the front door of the apartment, she wasn't surprised to see her father sitting quietly on the sofa, simply looking straight ahead, beyond the walls in front of him. It was as if he was looking beyond the life he found himself in to something much better.

"Dad?" she called out, knocking him out of his trance.

"Oh…hi, baby," he said to her, calmly. "How was school?"

"The same. Typical bullshit. Learning geometry and graphs and all the things that will be useless to me as an adult."

Jack couldn't help but chuckle.

She is wise far beyond her years.

"Well, you never know. Maybe you'll become an architect. Then you'll need it," he said.

"No way. I'm not going to be an architect. Fashion design. That's where it's at, man!

"Well then you're *definitely* going to have to learn that stuff," Jack said and laughed.

"Damn!" Jennifer said and laughed back.

"I guess you want to know why I'm home so early and sitting here like this," Jack said.

"Bad day at work?"

"That's putting it mildly, but yeah. Today I saw a man die in the Emergency Room. His face nearly chopped in half. Then later I was told that I wasn't collecting enough money from patients like this particular gentleman. That it would be in my best interest to ask him for some money before he spills any more blood on the floor," Jack told her.

"Holy shit. I hope you told those assholes where to stick it. You don't need them," Jennifer said angrily.

"I did. So now we're back at square one again, and I'm sorry."

"Don't worry about it, dad. You are so much better than that, and it hurts me to see you like this. I know you're struggling. I know you're in pain. Whatever happened five years ago must have been really horrible. Actually, I *know* it was horrible because you still won't tell me what happened. You'll have to tell me eventually, because that girl is back."

"Your girl....she's here and she's not alone...."

"Amanda," Jack finally said. A name he hoped would never again be spoken.

"Tell me what happened."

"Not now."

"If not now, WHEN?" Jennifer demanded.

"Soon. I promise. Let's just get some dinner."

CHAPTER 8

3:33 AM

Here we go again, must be "GHOST TIME" since 6:66 isn't possible.

Jennifer never awoke at 3:33. Once she opened her eyes and saw the time, she knew Amanda would soon be making another appearance. It was just a matter of when and how. The shock value had certainly diminished since the last visit, but the image of a young girl's rotted face was not something that she enjoyed seeing on a regular basis.

"I know you're there," Jennifer called out. "Why hide?"

"I'm sorry," a voice said at the foot of her bed. A young boy rose up and looked at her in a confused state.

"Who are you?" Jennifer asked.

"I'm Max. You're not scared of me, are you?" he asked her.

"No. Ghosts don't scare me. I know why you're here. You need something from me. From my father," she said.

"Yes," he answered.

"Hello, Jen," Amanda broke in, appearing directly next to Jennifer in her bed, and startling her just enough to make her fall out of it.

"God damn it, why do you have to do that?" Jennifer shouted.

"I'm a ghost, Jen. We don't knock on the door. We just appear and disappear whenever we want. We happen to prefer it this way."

"A ghost with a sense of humor. Nice," Jennifer chuckled.

"Well, I can't talk to you the same way I did when we were little kids. Well, *I'm* still a kid. You're not. You're going to have a long and fruitful life. Some of us, though…not so lucky. Show her, Max."

Max begins to unbutton his shirt, revealing a gaping hole in his chest where his heart had been removed.

"That's not my fault!" Jennifer shouted as tears began to roll down her eyes. "I know there are some evil fucking people in this world. People who kill little kids and get some sick pleasure from it, but I just don't see what any of this has to do with me."

"You have a higher purpose, Jennifer. Don't think that what you do here on Earth is the last word. The *be all and end all.* You have a divine task at hand."

"So just what are you trying to say to me? That God wants me to kill that scumbag in Texas? You really expect me to believe that? A peace-loving God who wants murder? And why doesn't He just do it himself? Or get you to do it? Just drop a radio in his bath water or something. Isn't that something a ghost would do?"

"Who said God is peace loving?" Amanda asked with a smirk.

"Well, isn't He?" Jennifer asked back, but Amanda just laughed. "You know, I just thought of something. Maybe you don't work for God. Maybe you work for the other guy."

"Really, Jennifer? You think that Hell is crawling with the souls of murdered children? And to answer your previous question…we can't kill anyone. We can manipulate environments, cause the occasional unexplained noise or disturbance, but that's it. Once they're in our world, though, then they're truly fucked."

"Nice language," Jennifer said and finally cracked a smile.

"Do I sound like a teenager?" Amanda asked.

"Hardly."

"Oh, well. I tried. It was funner when we just played with the tea set. It took a lot less effort."

"Even if I wanted to do what you asked, I don't think my dad will go along with it," Jennifer told Amanda.

"He will. After tonight, he's going to be a very different person."

"What are you going to do to him?" Jennifer asked, concerned.

"I'm not going to do anything. He's just going to see the truth. And anyone with even an ounce of a conscience will act. Your father has a big heart, and he *will* act."

· · · · ·

Like the eyes of an approaching monster, Jack could see two headlights in the distance approaching the farmhouse that stood behind him. Though the farmhouse looked about 100 years old, with moldy, rotting wood and a rusted tin roof, he still wanted to go inside. Anything would be better than waiting for whatever was approaching. But he couldn't move an inch, at least not until *he* arrived.

A white pickup truck pulled up and Jack watched as The Stranger grabbed what appeared to be a potato sack from the bed of the truck. He then took the sack and walked into the house, completely oblivious that Jack was watching his every move.

Jack now discovered that his legs were quite capable of moving, so he followed The Stranger into the house. They walked down a rather creaky wooden spiral staircase to the basement below, where The Stranger kept a rather large table, with a set of handcuffs attached to each of the four corners. He threw the bag onto the table where it landed with a loud thud.

Those aren't potatoes. That's for sure.

Suddenly a cell phone began to ring to the opening chords of Metallica's "Enter Sandman."

"Yeah?" The Stranger asked, but Jack couldn't hear the voice on the other end. "Yeah..yeah. I'm taking care of it now. You can come by later and do your thing."

Who the hell is he talking to? You mean there is a second person involved, for Christ's sake?

The sack of potatoes began to move, and a young frightful voice began to cry out.

"Mommy!"

"Hang on a sec," The Stranger said to the voice on the phone. He opened the sack to reveal a rather scared, five-year-old girl in a tutu.

"Make another sound and you die, and your mommy dies, too," he said to her quite calmly. He then quickly jumped back into his conversation. But the girl continued to cry, even louder than before.

DON'T YOU DARE FUCKING TOUCH HER, YOU MISERABLE EXCUSE FOR A HUMAN!

The Stranger walked over to the wall of the basement, where a set of tools were all lined up for him. He grabbed a large hammer and walked back towards the girl. Without much effort, he broke the girl's skull apart with one hit.

Jack fell to his knees, hopeless that he couldn't do a thing to help her. He soon realized that everything had been pre-programmed for him to see, and that's the way it was supposed to be. Yet, even though he had seen enough to convince him that this man deserved every ounce of pain coming to him, there was still more.

The Stranger walked over to the corner of the basement, where there was a desk with a laptop. As a river of blood began to pour around him, The Stranger powered up his laptop so he could sign on to Facebook.

Jack walked over to the desk as The Stranger signed in to his favorite site. He noticed a name on the left-hand side of the screen. It read: **ANTHONY MINER**, and below that, "**Edit Profile.**"

You're just dumb enough to use your own name, aren't you? I know who you are now, you fucking prick. Get ready, cause I'm coming for you.

With that, Jack awoke from his dream, and the first thing he saw when he opened his eyes was his daughter. He hugged her as hard as he had ever hugged her before, then began to cry.

CHAPTER 9

As the sun rose that morning, Jack paced the floor in the living room as though a million different ideas were running through his mind at the same time. Jennifer watched him patiently, wondering when he would finally let her in to his thought process.

"So…care to share some of those ideas with me?" she finally asked him.

"What time is it?" he asked back.

"Time? It's just after 6am," she replied.

"Turn on the news," he said. "I need to know."

"Know what?"

"Please, just do it," he demanded. She wasn't exactly sure why he cared so much about the news at this moment in time, but she did as he asked. The text at the bottom of the screen read: *A MOTHER'S ANGUISH.* A photo of young Gabriela Johnson was displayed on the left side of the screen. On the right was her mother, Rachel, a broken woman in pure agony. At least fifty reporters were pushing microphones into her face, hoping to catch some raw emotion that always plays well in the ratings.

"To the person who took my precious Gabby, I beg of you, please show mercy," Rachel cried. "She's only five years old. She has so much to live for. Please, please bring her home."

"Christ," Jack shouted. "I knew it. Turn it off."

"What, dad? What is it?" Jennifer asked him, turning off the TV.

"I saw that girl. In my dream."

"The one just now on TV?"

"Yeah. She's dead. He killed her, and I saw him do it. It was a dream, but it was a dream unlike any I've ever had. Everything was so clear, it was like someone was just playing a video in my head."

"That would have been Amanda," Jennifer said.

"You saw her again?"

"Yeah, and she told me that you were going to *see* the truth, and that once you saw it, you wouldn't be the same," she answered.

"How could anyone be?" Jack asked, not expecting a reply. "I think it's time I told you everything, Jennifer. It's been long enough."

CHAPTER 10

"When you were younger, we used to go on road trips once a year, sometimes for a weekend, sometimes a whole week. It kind of depended on your mother's mood at the time. Our last road trip together, we were up north near Shasta. As we were driving back home, and I remember it was really foggy at the time, we ran over a little girl in the road," Jack began.

"Amanda," Jennifer said.

"I picked her up, put her in the car, and attempted to get her to a hospital. She seemed all but dead, but then she started talking to you, and that's when the crash happened."

"Now *that* part I know about. *She* caused that?"

"Not really, no. I panicked when I heard her talking, and I crashed. The paramedics took us to the hospital, and there was no trace of Amanda anywhere. Everyone treated me like I was nuts just for suggesting that there was another person in the car," Jack continued.

"Well, you *did* just have a major traffic accident. I probably wouldn't have believed you either. I'd think you hit your head too hard," Jennifer said and laughed.

"Yeah, everyone assumed that, but I know what I saw that day. And after the accident, that's when you started acting strange. You started insisting that *you* were Amanda. It was as though somehow her spirit transferred to you when we were in that car."

"Which would probably explain why I don't remember a damn thing from that time," Jennifer said.

"I decided I wanted to find out who Amanda really was. I thought the only way I could help you was to find out the answers. So I drove out to the town where Amanda lived, and I met her mother."

"What was she like?" Jennifer asked.

"She was nice, actually. Really nice. Unfortunately, her brother wasn't so nice. When I found out that *he* was Amanda's killer, he tried to kill me. Thus the scars," Jack said, tapping on one of the two large marks on his face.

"Holy shit! So the killer was her uncle?"

"Actually, no. Her father. Well...I guess her uncle *and* her father," Jack explained.

"Wait a minute, I'm confused. Are you talking about some weird white-trash, incest situation? The brother and sister were Amanda's parents!?"

"Sadly, yes."

"That is some fucked up shit right there," Jennifer stated as only a teenager could.

"Amanda's mom saved me right at the last possible moment. The brother, Dwayne, had cut me up really bad. As he was about to end my life, she came in and blew his miserable fucking head off."

"Finally, some real justice!" Jennifer shouted.

"And then she turned the gun on herself."

"Wait..what?"

"She killed herself. She couldn't take the guilt anymore. She knew her brother was a killer, and she covered up for him from day one."

"That's sad. But I'm glad she saved you," Jennifer said and smiled.

"I am, too," Jack said. "After that, I went to see you again. I was hoping that everything would finally be okay. You were at the psychiatrists office and I walked in. You didn't say anything at first. You just kept looking at me and smiling. I wasn't sure who you were. I kept saying 'Is this Jennifer or Amanda?' and then finally, after what seemed like an enternity, you said 'daddy' and I knew it was you. That you were back. And up until recently the name Amanda had never even crossed your lips."

"Wow. I have no memory of any of that," Jennifer said.

"Consider yourself lucky. I wish I could shield you from all the evil in this world, but I've realized that's an impossibility. When one monster is put down, another one always pops up. This…animal…in Texas. He kills little children. I saw him bash that girl's skull with a hammer like he was cracking an egg, and he thought nothing of it. I know why Amanda wanted me to see it. She wants me to kill the guy, and if anyone deserves to be put down, it's this guy. But what I haven't figured out is what the connection is between *this* guy and Amanda. It doesn't fit the whole *ghost logic!*" Jack explained.

"Ghost logic? Are you saying ghosts are logical?" Jennifer asked him, amused.

"In a way, yes. I mean…I think they are. A ghost is all about unfinished business. A person dies in a bad way, before their time. They want answers, or in some cases, they want revenge."

"There was a second ghost last night. The little boy, Max. She was with Amanda. He was one of the victims of the Texas guy," Jennifer told him.

Your girl…she's here and she's not alone.

"That's it. The guy with the machete in his face at the hopital. He must have seen them."

"Wait a minute, you lost me. The guy with the machete in his face?"

"He said 'your girl is here and she's not alone.' He must have been talking about Amanda and Max. But then he started talking about 'Room 17.' Does that mean anything to you?" Jack asked her.

"Room 17? I have no idea. That could be anything. Maybe the guy was late for class, Room 17 was health ed. or biology or something."

"Okay, let's just forget about that one for now. But you see, it makes absolute sense that that boy would want revenge. *That* makes sense. Of course he wants to see this guy ground into hamburger, but again, what is Amanda doing with him?

"Maybe they became friends in the Ghost World. Maybe the afterlife isn't all that different than it is here. Friends still look out for each other," Jennifer explained, but Jack wasn't buying it.

"Really? The *Ghost World?* If this is what the afterlife is like, then I'm really fucking depressed."

"Hey, I'm just putting stuff out there to see what sticks. So the Amanda/Texas psycho connection is something we have to figure out. In the meantime, what is our next move?"

"Well, I've got one pretty good piece of information. I know his name," Jack said.

"Are you serious?" Jennifer asked him, shocked.

"Yep, and have a pretty good idea how to find him."

"You got all this from your dream?"

"Yeah, which is why it's pretty much useless to anyone else but me. No one would believe me. Trust me, I've been through this before. You go into a police station and start telling the police about your dreams, *you're* the one who's likely to get locked up," Jack said.

"So if you find him, you'll just kill him. Just like that? We're talking about Texas here. They'll execute you if you just kill a man in cold blood."

"You don't think I know that? Obviously I have to find proof, and draw him out. If I get him panicked enough, he'll come to me, and then I'll get him."

"Sounds dangerous yet exciting. Count me in," Jennifer said.

"I'd prefer you sit this one out, Jen. Like you said, it's dangerous, and I've seen what this guy can do."

"No fucking way, dad. I'm with you. We're a team. You're not going anywhere without me," Jennifer insisted.

"I'll let you come if you promise me one thing. When the time comes when I have to face him, I don't want you there. I never want you to be close to him. Got it?"

"Of course."

"Good," Jack said.

"So," Jennifer began. "You ready for another road trip?"

CHAPTER 11

PALM GROVE, CA, 15 YEARS EARLIER

Anthony Miner knew that this birthday was going be special. It was his 21st, and when his best friend, Dwayne Grimmits, drove up to take him out, an excitement lit up inside him like he had just reunited with a lost love.

"You ready, buddy?" Dwanye asked him.

"Fuck yeah I am. Where we goin?"

"I told ya, dickface. It's a surprise."

They drove for some time. If it was action you were looking for, you had to get as far away from Pine Grove as possible, and Dwayne knew exactly where to go. Bella Vista was a hell hole, but it was Dwayne's kind of hell hole. At night, the place became a regular hangout for meth heads, drug dealers, and prostitutes. You could get anything you want at a very reasonable price, and Dwayne was there to eye Tony's birthday present.

"What the fuck you bring me to Crack Town USA for?" Tony asked.

"You're gonna lose your cherry tonight, my friend."

"Shit. For real?"

"Absolutely. You see that little piece of ass over there?" Dwayne said and pointed at a young girl who looked about 18 standing under a street light. "That's the one you're going to fuck tonight."

Dwanye pulled his truck alongside the girl, who still had a baby face and looked like she'd rather be anywhere else. She had long black hair and a good figure. She was pretty, which suggested she hadn't been working the street for that long.

"Hey, babe. What can I get ya?" she shouted into the truck.

"It's my friend's birthday today. I wanted to get him somethin' special," Dwayne said.

"Hey, happy birthday, guy. I can give you my birthday special. One hundred bucks."

"That's your *birthday* special? Kind of a lot, don't you think?" Dwayne asked her and laughed.

"You get what you pay for. You can fuck the skanks down the street if you want bargain basement."

"How bout I give you a hundred fifty, but for both of us. That's seventy five a piece. Not bad money for about one hour's work," Dwayne said.

"All right, you got a deal," she said.

"What's your name, anyway?" Tony asked.

"Krystal," she said.

"Well, Krystal. Hop on in here."

· · · · ·

When Krystal noticed that Dwayne had passed every available motel and began to drive on a small dirt road, she knew something wasn't right. If she knew just who her customers were, she would have run. But with youth comes naivete, and she thought these two just looked like typical young, horny guys.

"You passed all the motels. I don't go for this backwoods stuff," she told them.

"The police are always watching those motels. They'll put all three of us in jail. You don't want that, do you? Not on my friend's birthday. No fucking way," Dwayne explained. "Besides, we're here."

He stopped the car, leaving the headlights on.

"My friend first. Then me," Dwayne told her.

"Where do you want to do it? In the back of the truck?" Krystal asked.

"No. Behind it. Doggy style," Dwayne said.

"Do you ever let your friend talk?"

"I'm good with doggy style," Tony said. The three of them got out of the truck and walked to the back. Krystal pulled down her pants and placed her hands on the back of the truck.

"Let's get this over with," she said.

"Fuck, can you try to sound at least a little fucking excited?" Dwayne shouted.

"Ok," she said and began to mimick a porn actress. "Come on, baby. Give it to me good and hard. I'm waiting."

Dwayne looked over at Tony, who was simply standing there looking at the girl's body.

"Well, what are you waiting for, dumb ass? Whip it out and give it to her. We ain't got all night."

Tony walked over to the girl and pulled down his pants, revealing an embarrassingly flaccid, small member.

"I can't...um...I can't...." Tony began.

"You can't get it up?" Dwayne asked him and laughed. "Holy shit, man. You got a beautiful naked girl here in front of you and you can't get it up?"

"I don't know. I'm nervous," he said.

"You ain't gay, are ya? Please don't tell me that you're some motherfuckin' faggot."

"I ain't no fag, man," Tony said.

"Try playin' with it. That might get it workin'."

"It's just not happening, man," Tony told him. Krystal looked over at them and sighed.

"Are we done here, then?" she asked them.

"Fuck no," Dwayne said. "I'm gonna show this boy how it's done."

Dwayne pulled down his pants and entered her from behind. With each thrust harder than the last, any feelings of pleasure the girl had at the beginning were turning to pain.

"It hurts," she yelled.

"Shut the fuck up," Dwayne shouted back and within about a minute, he had come.

"Asshole," she whispered under her breath. She began to reach for her panties, but before she could lift them, Dwayne had pulled a knife from a holster around his ankle and lunged it into her side, piercing her kidney. A spray of blood flew from the wound and didn't let up. A fatal wound, to be sure.

"Holy shit, man!" Tony shouted, surprised and excited at the same time. The young girl collapsed to the ground with not even enough strength to utter a single scream.

"Do her a favor and finish her off," Dwayne told him and handed him his blood-stained knife. Tony took the knife and straddled the girl, who just looked at him helpless.

"Now I know why you couldn't get it up," Krystal whispered to him. "This is what really gets you off, isn't it?"

Tony raised the knife and brought it down on her again and again and again. It was his first taste of blood, and he loved it.

CHAPTER 12

I see the bad moon arising

I see trouble on the way

I see earthquakes and lightnin'

I see bad times today

Don't go around tonight

Well, it's bound to take your life

There's a bad moon on the rise

After more than 8 hours on the road, Jack and Jennifer had just crossed into New Mexico on Interstate 10. Jennifer had just about reached her threshold of classic rock radio.

"Can we please listen to something else now?" she pleaded with her father.

"Really? You don't like CCR? 'Fortunate Son', 'Run Through the Jungle', 'Proud Mary', 'Suzie Q', 'Down on the Corner'? None of those do anything for you?" Jack asked her, as he was a proud aficionado of all things classic rock.

"'Down the on the Corner'. Yeah, that's the Walgreens commerical. That one's kinda cool. I didn't know it was the same band."

"You need help, girl. Serious help. Let's consider this road trip a course in Classic Rock 101," Jack said with a smile. "How about some Springsteen next?"

"Please, no Springsteen. The guy always sings like a vein is going to burst through his forehead," Jennifer said, laughing.

"You gotta go before *Born in the USA* and all the later stuff. Listen to *Born to Run.* 'Jungleland' is absolute perfection," Jack explained.

"No, thanks. I'd rather stick to the present decade if you don't mind," Jennifer said.

"Oh, come on. Do you know how many writers it takes to create these pop songs today? A Miley Cyrus or Katy Perry or Justin Bieber..." Jack started.

"Hey...I never said I liked Just Bieber," Jennifer interrupted.

"Okay...whatever. Like I was saying, these so called singers today need an entire *team* of writers to create their latest hit song. Do you know how many writers Bruce Springsteen uses for his albums? Do you know how many writers wrote 'Bohemian Rhapsody'?"

"I have no idea, but I guess you're going to tell me anyway."

"One. One single writer. Now you've got a team of writers, you got singers who can't actually sing a note and have to rely on all this auto-tuning technology just to sing in tune. There aren't any real artists anymore. It's all corporate product created on an assembly line," Jack said, and Jennifer just laughed. She knew it was true, but didn't really care.

"Okay, old man. You off your soap box now?" she asked with a smile.

"Absolutely," Jack said and laughed with her.

"I'm getting a bit tired. Can we stop in the next town?" Jennifer asked with a yawn.

"Sure. I saw a sign for a town called Lordsburg up ahead. It's not much further."

· · · · ·

After checking in at the Econo Inn, which was indeed cheap (but the very definition of the phrase "you get what you pay for") they endured the worst Chinese food ever at a locally owned restaurant known simply as The China Inn. The owners, immigrants from China no less, thought Americans couldn't stomach the taste of *real* Chinese food, so they smothered every dish in brown gravy.

"Well, don't expect high quality cuisine in a one-horse town in New Mexico," Jack said to Jennifer when she informed him that she may be inclined to vomit within the next hour. On the other side of the highway, a little shop called Eye of the Cat caught Jennifer's attention. Below the name it read:

PSYCHIC READINGS

READER & ADVISOR

$10 SPECIAL : PALM AND TAROT CARD

WALK INS WELCOME

"Dad, can we do that? Please, please, please?" she begged him.

"Psychic readings? You really want to add *more* paranormal crap to our lives? As if we don't have enough already?"

"Oh, come on. These people are just entertainers. I've always wanted to go to one."

"Fine. But this will have to come out of tomorrow's dinner budget. Instead of greasy Chinese, it will be cheese and crackers with juice," Jack told her.

"Deal," Jennifer said.

· · · · ·

As they opened the door, an overpowering smell of burning incense struck them immediately. The top of the door struck some overhead chimes, alerting the owner that someone had entered. The living room was dimly lit with candles, and a reading table was centered in the middle of the room.

"Sorry, we're closed," a female voice called out from another room. "The store closed about ten minutes ago."

"Aww, damn it! Too late," Jennifer said, frustrated.

An older woman in her early 60's with long, raggedy gray hair appeared from the other room. She wore a flashy pink blouse covered by at least half a dozen large bead necklaces.

"Where are you folks from?" she asked them.

"California," Jack answered. "We're on our way to Texas. It was my daughter's idea to come here, but we'll get going."

"Hold on just a second," the woman said and extended her hand to Jennifer. They looked at each other as though they were experiencing a sense of *déjà vu.* "My name is Mae. What's yours?"

"Jennifer," she answered and took Mae's hand.

"Very nice to meet you, Miss Jennifer. And your name, sir?"

"Jack. Jack Taylor."

"Nice to meet you, too," Mae said and shook Jack's hand as well.

"So, you're open or closed?" Jack asked her.

"I don't want to disappoint your daughter. I think I can squeeze the two of you in. You'll be my last customers for the night," Mae told them.

"We don't want to inconvenience you or anything," Jack said, clearly trying to talk his way out of it.

"Not at all. When I walked into this room, your daughter gave off the most spiritual energy I have ever felt. I've seen thousands of people, Mr. Taylor, and I've never, *ever* had these sorts of vibes that I'm feeling now," Mae explained.

"That's a good thing then, isn't it?" Jack asked.

"Please, sit down. Would you like any tea?" Mae asked them.

"No, we're fine. We just had dinner," Jack said and the two of them sat down behind the table. Mae moved the reading table, pulled up a chair and sat between them.

"Now Jennifer, if you don't mind, may you give me your hand again?"

"Hold on one second," Jack interrupted. "Before you start, can you tell me what you're going to charge us for this."

"Dad. Please," Jennifer said to him, embarassed.

"I just don't want to have any big surprises later on," Jack explained.

"Don't worry, Mr. Taylor. There's no charge today. Now...Miss Jennifer, if you don't mind?"

As Jennifer extended her hand to Mae, the old psychic looked up to the ceiling and then closed her eyes.

"You've come on a long journey, and it's not finished yet," Mae began.

No shit. We already told you we're from California. Tell me something I don't know.

"However...someone is following you," she continued.

"Who? Someone bad?" Jack asked.

"No. Not bad, but not good either. Someone I would say doesn't have your best interests at heart."

Vague. So fucking vague. Typical fake psychic.

"I see a lot of pain on this journey that you've embarked on. But with this pain will come an awakening," Mae continued.

"What kind of pain? And what awakening?" Jack asked, doubtful.

"Your daughter's awakening. Her gift," Mae said.

"What gift?"

"Mr. Taylor. You must know. You really take me for a charlatan?"

"Aren't most of the people in your profession?"

"I'm not," Mae said. "When did she start seeing visions?"

"When she was five," Jack said.

"Interesting," Mae continued. "And moving objects?"

"What? She's never…" Jack started.

"How did you know that?" Jennifer interrupted.

"Well, I wouldn't say moving. Destroying would be a better word," Mae said. "Your daughter has quite a talent, Mr. Taylor. A talent unlike any I've ever seen. It will save her life. Maybe yours, too."

"Jen, were you ever going to tell me about this?" Jack asked her.

"In time, Dad. I still haven't figured it out myself," Jennifer answered.

"And what about the pain you're talking about?" Jack asked Mae. "Are we in physical danger if we continue this trip?"

"It's hard to see. You haven't told me why you're going to Texas, but I can tell it's not for a family reunion or to eat barbeque ribs."

"We're going to stop a child killer," Jack said rather bluntly.

"So, it's about revenge then. Well, Mr. Taylor, I'll tell you something, and I'm sure you've heard it many times before, but it's such a great quote that it always bears repeating: *Before you embark on a journey of revenge, dig two graves.*"

CHAPTER 13

The Stranger, who had now been identified by at least one person as Mr. Anthony Miner, watched the schoolyard from his truck across a busy intersection. He had no intention of grabbing any kids from the playground. He knew that would be outright suicidal. He simply liked to *watch*. And when he wasn't thinking about killing, he was *watching*. As he watched the children playing on the slides and the swings and the monkey bars, he slowly began to put one hand down his pants.

"Yeah…that's it," he said to himself with a moan, but was interrupted by the sound of a loud horn.

"Hey, buddy! You can't park there! That's a loading and unloading zone!" a voice shouted at him from a large white van. The driver hadn't seen Mr. Miner's indiscretions. If he had, Mr. Miner likely would have been arrested immediately, and events would have been set in motion that would have exposed Miner's homicidal history. This was often how serial killers had been caught. Not because of bravado police work, but because the killer was caught with a broken tail light or masturbating in the front seat. It wasn't to be the case this time.

"Sorry about that," Miner shouted back to the man and started his truck. Without looking, he quickly pulled into traffic, not noticing the giant school bus just a few feet away and traveling at 40 mph towards him.

The brakes on the bus screeched with a deafening roar but struck Miner's truck directly on the driver's side. He wasn't wearing a seat belt, and the impact of the bus sent him flying to the other side of the truck, bashing his head into the passenger's side window.

The driver of the bus, an old Chinese man who spoke little English, got out and ran over to the mangled truck to check on the driver, who he assumed he had killed. The bus was completely full with schoolchildren, and all of them wanted to look, some of them even attempting to get off the bus to get closer.

"GET BACK ON BUS!" the Chinese man shouted at them. The bus had sustained very little damage, and the kids were all fine. Rather, they seemed excited at being part of a crash site. The bus driver looked at the bloody mess of a man in the truck and put his hand on his forehead, as if to say: *I've just killed this guy. I'm going to lose my job.*

"Hey, man. I saw everything. It wasn't your fault. That guy just pulled out in front of you without even looking," the man driving the white van said to him.

"Please call police."

CHAPTER 14

Three-year-old Amanda Grimmits had been sleeping quietly when she heard her uncle, Dwayne, and his best friend, Tony, pull up outside of her house. Her mother, Joanne, had already passed out for the evening on about 8 shots of vodka and wasn't about to be waking up anytime soon. Amanda looked out her bedroom window and saw them carrying a large sack into the backyard.

"I got a couple of shovels in the shed," Dwayne said to Tony.

"How deep we gotta dig?" Tony asked him.

"Pretty fuckin' deep, man. You don't want some fuckin' animal comin' around and diggin' up this shit, do you? It's gotta be like at least six feet."

"Fuck! That's gonna take all night," Tony complained.

"You want we should just leave her here? Spread eagle for the world to see? Yeah, that sounds like a good idea…if I wanna go to the fuckin' gas chamber."

"Sorry."

As the two men began to dig, little Amanda walked out into the backyard to see what they were doing.

"What's that?" she asked Dwayne, pointing at the bloody sack in front of them.

"Holy shit! Who is that?" Tony asked.

"Don't worry about it. It's just my niece, Amanda," Dwayne said. "Now, Amanda. You know you ain't supposed to be out here this late. Your uncle has got some important business he's got to do, and his friend, Tony, is gonna help him. Now just go back to bed, and tomorrow I'll take you out for ice cream."

"Is that a dead animal?" she asked.

"Yeah. We hit a deer coming home. It's a real mess. Very bloody. You don't wanna see it," Dwayne told her.

"Yuck!" Amanda exclaimed.

"Exactly. Yuck!" Dwayne said back. "Now good night, Amanda."

"Good night," she said and walked to her room. She would see them again in her backyard from time to time, always with another bag, and eventually it just became routine.

CHAPTER 15

In the small town of Comfort, Texas, which was just Northwest of San Antonio, Jack and Jennifer stopped for their second night. They were starving, and the only place they could walk to from their hotel was a dive of a restaurant called Dick's Bar & Grill. Though the place was mostly filled with bar patrons, the manager agreed to serve Jennifer as long as the two of them sat at the table that was the farthest away from the bar.

"I can see you two look exhausted. What can I get for ya?" the waiter asked.

"You Dick?" Jack asked.

"That's me. Proud owner of this fine establishment. Where ya'll from?"

"California," Jennifer answered.

"California. We get lots of California people coming out here. Economy and all. Actually, regardless of what you might hear, Texans love Californians. We love your business. As long as you only visit and don't stay," Dick said, laughing. "Just kidding."

"We don't plan on staying that long," Jack said.

"I'm just messin' with ya. Stay as long as you want. So let me tell you what's good here. We got some fine barbeque ribs. We also got some deep fried catfish. Or, if you like it simple, we got spaghetti or hamburgers."

"Hamburgers sound fine. Make it two," Jack said.

"Comin' right up," Dick said proudly.

"Make mine a cheeseburger," Jennifer said.

"You got it, little lady!" Dick said and disappeared to the kitchen.

"Seems like a nice guy," Jennifer said.

"He's what they call *Texas friendly*."

"What does that mean?" Jennifer asked.

"Just a reputation Texas people seem to have. That they're all friendly," Jack answered.

"Is that true, though? I mean, everything I've heard about Texas isn't exactly positive. Isn't this the place where they want to let students carry guns in schools? And not let gay people get married?" Jennifer asked.

"They just have some rather old fashioned ideas. Not to say that it's bad. It's just…different."

"Texas is a shithole," a voice called out from behind them. An older gentleman with a goatee approached them, a beer in hand. "Outside of Austin, these people are still living a hundred years in the past."

Jack laughed as the man walked up to their table.

"And who are you?" Jack asked.

"Allow me to introduce myself. My name is Mr. Lawrence Phillips. I'm a scientist. I'm here for a convention in Austin. If it wasn't for Austin, which I love, I would completely write this state off. Do you mind if I have a seat?"

Jack quickly looked him over and decided that, because of his age, he wasn't likely a threat.

He may be a dirty old man, for all I know, but he also looks weak and slow. He looks like an old nerd, actually. Maybe we can argue the pros and cons of Kirk and Picard.

"And your name, my good man?" Mr. Phillips.

"Jack. Jack Taylor."

"And this must be your beautiful daughter?"

Jennifer began to blush and looked over at her father, who was beginning to feel a bit uncomfortable.

"This is Jennifer," Jack said.

"Pleasure to meet you, Jennifer Taylor," he said in his eloquent style.

"So…not a lover of Texas, huh? I take it you're not a conservative," Jack implied.

"I'm a lover of education and science. I'm someone who believes climate change is real. I support equal rights for all, and especially support a woman's right to do whatever the hell she wants to with her body. So, I guess you can say no, I'm not a conservative." Mr. Phillips replied.

"You better keep those opinions tight lipped around here," Jack said.

"Yes. Especially in an establishment such as this. I'd prefer not to get beat within an inch of my life," Mr. Phillips stated and the two men laughed.

This guy is funny. A little bit prissy. But funny.

"So you said you're a scientist? What kind of scientist?" Jennifer asked him.

"I'm a parapsychologist. Specifically, I study something that's called *psychokinesis.*"

"What's that?" Jennifer asked him, her interest suddenly sparked.

"It's a very special ability. One of which very, very few people actually possess. It's an ability to move or deform inanimate objects by simply the power of the mind," Mr. Phillips explained.

"Have you ever met such a person?" Jack asked, wondering just how random this encounter with Mr. Phillips really was.

"Once, quite some time ago, our organization put up an offer of a million dollars to anyone who could prove that they had this ability. We saw literally hundreds of people, including some Hollywood celebrities, believe it or not," he began.

"Why does that not surprise me?" Jack asked with a smile.

"Well, needless to say, not one of them actually possessed the slightest bit of any sort of talent. It was a waste of time and resources. What I learned from all of that, however, was that those who truly possess this gift, see it as a curse, and they don't want anyone to know about it. Whether for one million or fifty million dollars, they just want to remain in the shadows. And can you blame them?"

"What would you do with someone like that if you found them?" Jennifer asked.

"We only want to help them. To help them understand their power, and to control it."

"Well, it sounds like you have an impossible search ahead of you there, Mr. Phillips," Jack said, hoping to end this conversation. As luck would have it, their hamburgers had arrived just at the right time.

"One hamburger, and one cheeseburger for the little lady!" Dick said with a giant grin. "What about you, sir? Anything I can get for you?"

"The beer is just fine, my good man. Actually, for a local beer, I'm impressed," Mr. Phillips said.

"That's *Shiner* beer. The best beer in Texas, and the best yer likely to find anywhere else in the world," Dick said proudly.

"It's good, I'll give you that. But I suggest you pay a visit to a little town called Königsberg."

"Where's that? Near Lubbock?" Dick asked him.

"That's in Germany. The greatest beer I've ever tasted was in Königsberg."

"Well, I don't know nuthin' about no kraut beer. But if it's good as you say, bring me some and I'll tell you what I think," Dick told him. "Kraut beer or no kraut beer, if it's good, I'll serve it."

"Very well. If I ever make my way into the armpit of Texas again, I'll bring one," Mr. Phillips said rather bluntly.

"Pfffft!" Dick said and walked away.

A young boy, about 18 and with pimples on about every inch of his face, approached their table.

"Hey, girlie," he said, looking at Jennifer. "You wanna dance?"

"You're kidding, right?" Jennifer asked back.

"Nah, I ain't kiddin'. You wanna dance?" the boy asked again.

"How old are you, kid?" Jack asked him. "She's only thirteen, you know."

"It's just dancin'. No harm done. What do you say, girl? You comin'?" the boy insisted.

"Nah, I don't think so," Jennifer answered.

"Come on. Just one dance. What are you afraid of?"

"I'm not afraid of anything. Certainly not you," Jennifer said.

"Look, she said no," Jack said.

"I ain't talkin' to you, old man," the boy said. He appeared to have had one too many drinks.

"Well, this old man happens to be her father," Jack said, his patience starting to grow thin.

"Ah, I get it. Y'all are a couple of fags, and this is your adopted daughter, right? Two old fucking queers with a hot chick for a daughter you know you'd never want to fuck."

"I'd listen to him if I were you," Mr. Phillips told the boy.

"Shut the fuck up, old man. You've been sucking so much cock your face has turned into a fucking prune."

"Why don't you look at your own face," Jennifer said to the boy. "I can play fucking connect-the-dots with your ugly mug."

"You got a mouth on you, girl. I'm gonna wash it out for you with my dick juice," the boy said.

The *dick juice* comment was the last straw for Jack, who got up from his seat and looked at the boy as though he was one more word from losing a tooth.

"If you don't get the fuck away from us in three seconds, your face is going to hit the ground so hard that all your zits will burst in one big, pus-filled explosion."

"Okay, calm down, Scarface. I can see you're an O.G. It's all good," the boy said and walked away.

"Can we get out of here, dad?" Jennifer asked her father.

"Yeah, bring your burger with you. We'll eat it at the hotel."

"I think I'll be on my way as well," Mr. Phillips said.

"Probably a good idea," Jack said.

・ ・ ・ ・ ・

As the three left the restaurant into the parking lot, a group of four large men, along with the pimply boy, ran out to meet them. Jack could see the combined IQ of the four men was about 50, so he knew that reasoning with them would not be much of an option. He felt sorry for Mr. Phillips, since he was now caught up in this as well.

"Hey, faggots!" one man shouted. He looked to be in his early 20's, very well built. He may have been a star on the local football team, but was now bitter since the only job he could get was at the nearby car wash. "Yeah, you two faggots! Where ya goin?"

"What do you want, anyway?" Jack asked him, knowing the response would be something completely asinine.

"I hear you threatened my little brother. I can't have no fag going around here making threats. It gives us a bad reputation," the man said.

"And beating up people you think are gay *doesn't* give you a bad reputation?" Mr. Phillips asked him.

"Fuck no. Makes me feel good," the man said. "So we're gonna kick the shit out of you two queers, and then my little brother is gonna get his dance with your girl. He might want to fuck her when he's done, but that's his business."

"You put your hand on her, and this is the last day you will have air in your lungs," Jack said, clenching his fist.

"Big talk from a faggot. Let's get these guys," the man said and they began to fight. Jack threw the first bunch, hitting the ex-football player and knocking him hard to the ground. The other three began to attack Mr. Phillips, who had very little trouble keeping them off. He fought them back like a man who had been trained in hand-to-hand combat. He was a bit rusty, not having used such skills in at least 20 years, but it came back to him rather quickly. Jack, on the other hand, wasn't doing quite so well. The ex-football player soon got up and landed a hard blow to Jack's face, knocking him over. Once he fell, the man straddled him and began to pound on his face in a fit of violent rage.

"Stop it!" Jennifer screamed. "Get off him!" She grabbed the man's face and scratched it, but he pushed her aside.

"Get the fuck off me!" the ex-football player said to Jennifer, and he continued to pound away.

"I said STOP IT!" she shouted again and suddenly the man felt a violent force strike his nose, as if a man with an iron fist had just laid a devastating blow. The man's nose began to sink into his face, a wild spray of blood shooting into the air.

"Arrrrrrrrrrrrrrrggggggggggggggggghhhhhhh!" the man screamed, holding his severely broken nose. "What in the fuck did you do to me?" he asked in an incredibly nasal tone. Jennifer just looked at him silently. She turned to Mr. Phillips, who stood above three unconscious men. The pimply boy, seeing his posse bleeding profusely and/or unconscious, ran away rather quickly.

"Help me, please," she said to Mr. Phillips.

· · · · ·

Jennifer opened the hotel room door and Mr. Phillips helped carry Jack into the room and onto the bed. He had been beat unconscious.

"Keep an eye on him tonight. If he has any trouble breathing, roll him over on his side. That will help. He took quite a beating, but it doesn't look that bad. He should feel a little better by morning. Sore, but better," Mr. Phillips told her.

"How the hell did you beat up those three guys? You took them down like they were nothing. I thought you were just a scientist. What are you, some kind of ninja scientist or something?"

"No," Mr. Phillips laughed. "I was in the military some time ago. You never really forget your training. Those men only know one style of fighting. Brute force. Once you can predict every punch they're going to throw, it's easy to defend."

"Well, I was impressed," Jennifer said.

"Nothing to it, actually. What about you? I saw something rather unusual, Jennifer. You broke that man's nose, didn't you?

"I don't know what happened. I starting shouting at him, and the next thing I know his nose is bleeding," she explained. Mr. Phillips smiled.

"You know you have a gift, don't you?" he asked her.

"Everyone keeps saying that. How can it be a gift when I don't even know what it is or how to control it?"

"I can help you. Like I told you, this is my area of expertise. I've been looking for someone like you all my life, Jennifer. I wasn't sure you were real until tonight. Most of my leads always end up cold," Mr. Phillips told her.

"What are you talking about?" Jennifer asked.

"Come with me, Jennifer," Mr. Phillips said and very gently put his hand on her leg. "I can help you to understand and control your power. You'll never be afraid again."

"I'm going to have to ask you to leave," Jennifer said. "I need to take care of my dad."

"Absolutely," Mr. Phillips said. He had no intention to cross a girl that he knew could be a human nutcracker. "Let me give you my card. If you ever need someone to talk to, you can reach me at this number 24/7."

"Thanks," Jennifer said and took the card. Mr. Phillips began to leave, but looked at her once more.

"Are you sure I can't do any more for you?" he asked.

"No, you've done enough, and I appreciate all your help. I need to be with my dad now."

"Okay. Good luck on your trip," Mr. Phillips said to her and left the room. He proceeded to walk to his car and began entering numbers on his cell phone.

"It's me," he said into the phone. "This one is a go."

As he hung up the phone, a large man with a crowbar smashed the window next to him.

"Faggot, you just beat up a bunch of my friends. You're gonna pay with your a…" the man began, but before he could finish, Mr. Phillips had drawn a 640 Smith & Wesson revolver and put a bullet between the man's eyes.

CHAPTER 16

Jack awoke the next morning in intense pain. He knew he had taken a pretty hard beating, but the pain hadn't really set in until he awoke.

"You're awake," Jennifer said, smiling. She thought maybe he would have been out much longer.

"What happened?" he asked her. His memory was a bit fuzzy, and he wondered how he ended up back in the hotel room.

"You and Mr. Phillips got into a fight with those rednecks at the bar," she explained. "One guy beat you pretty bad."

"The last thing I remember was getting hit in the face and falling on my ass. Everything went black after that. How about Mr. Phillips? How is he?"

"Mr. Phillips? I'll say, for an old guy, he's got some moves. He took out three of them," Jennifer told him.

"What?" Jack asked, surprised. "You're kidding, right?"

"Nope. Old guy worked 'em like a navy seal or something."

"What the hell?"

"I kept checking the window all night. A bunch of police showed up at the restaurant about thirty minutes later. They were there for a while until some black vans showed up. Then everybody left. I was a little worried they were going to take me away," Jennifer said.

"Take you away? Why?" Jack asked.

"I hurt one of them," she answered. "The guy who was hitting you. I hurt him. Bad."

"How bad?" Jack asked.

"Broke his nose, I think. Creep deserved it," Jennifer said.

"You broke his nose? The guy was six feet and over two hundred pounds, how could you…" Jack started but stopped himself, realizing that maybe it was Jennifer's *gift*.

"It just happened. I couldn't really control it," she explained.

"Listen, Jennifer. This power you have. It's something I don't understand. Call it a gift from God, or a gift from some other supernatural entity, I don't know. I'll never fully understand that stuff. But one thing I do understand is the nature of man. If you show this talent of yours to anyone, there are people out there who will want to exploit you. They'll use you for their own sadistic purposes. Man has a history of taking things that are pure and good and destroying it for their own selfishness. You have to hide this inside you and never let it out," Jack explained.

"But that man. I didn't want him to hurt you. He could have killed you," Jennifer said, beginning to cry.

"I appreciate that, but I can take care of myself," he said. "However…if you ever find yourself in a situation where it's either you or the other guy, you do what you have to to survive."

"Okay, dad. I will," she said, crying, and the two hugged each other.

"Okay, okay. We're getting too emotional now," Jack said, wiping a tear from his eye. "Let's see if they're talking about us on the news this morning."

Jack walked over to the television and turned on the local news. Not a word about the redneck bar fight in Comfort, Texas, but rather, something else that disturbed Jack even more. The headline at the bottom read:

DAVIS ELEMENTARY SCHOOL STARTS FUNDRAISER FOR INJURED MAN

"Thirty seven year old Anthony Miner, who, as we reported earlier, was struck by a Davis Elementary School bus and is listed in critical but stable condition, found himself blessed by a guardian angel. Five hundred and forty two of them to be exact, as the school has now begun a fundraiser to help pay for Mr. Miner's medical bills, which are sure to be in the hundreds of thousands, as he apparently has no medical insurance," the reporter said.

"I felt really bad for him," a six-year old student said, "and our bus driver, too. I saw him crying when he got back on the bus. I think he felt sad or something."

"NO!" Jack shouted at the television. "No, no, no, no, no! This can't be happening."

"The doctors here at St. Paul's North Austin Medical Center have told us that they expect Mr. Miner to have a full recovery, but it will take some time. Lots of time. For KEYE TV, this is Mandy Mitchell!"

"We've got to go there," Jack said and turned off the television.

CHAPTER 17

In just a little over two hours, Jack and Jennifer had entered Austin, Texas. They checked themselves into an Extended Stay hotel on the north side of town, which didn't look so crime-ridden as some of the other areas they had passed. Jack, still exhausted and recovering from the previous night, decided he needed some rest before he could do anything else. He collapsed onto his bed with a loud grunt of relief.

"So what now?" Jennifer asked.

"First we get some rest. Then I'm gonna try to talk to our friend over there at St. Paul's," Jack answered.

"You're just going to go right up to him. Just like that?" Jennifer asked.

"People don't know he's a psychotic child killer. It's not like he's being guarded or anything. Remember, I worked at a hospital. You'd be amazed how poor security is. As long as you have a badge, you can go anywhere you want. People don't even look. There's so many different departments and different uniforms, it's easy to blend in."

"But you don't even have a badge," Jennifer said.

"Yes, I do. I never turned in my old one from my last job. It's in the car, along with the uniform."

"It doesn't matter that it doesn't match?"

"No. Like I told you, all you have to do is *look* like you belong there. Unless it's a high profile patient or celebrity, nobody gives a shit," Jack said.

"Whatever you say. And when you find him?" Jennifer asked.

"I'm going to try to get whatever information I can. Anything that will help get this guy locked up for the rest of his life."

"You're not going to kill him, then," Jennifer said, relieved.

"As shitty as security is, you can't just kill someone at a hospital and expect to just walk out. Someone will notice. And I need to know for sure that it's really him. What do we have as proof so far? Ghosts and dreams? That won't stand up in court."

"You're right. I want to come with you," Jennifer said.

"No. I need you to stay here. It'll be much easier for me to work my way through that hospital alone rather than bringing along a thirteen-year-old kid. As soon as I get something…anything…I'll come back," Jack told her.

"Fine. Just be careful."

"But now I just need a little sleep…just a little slee…" Jack said and drifted away. He slept for the next eight hours.

CHAPTER 18

As Jack walked into St. Paul's North Austin Medical Center, he knew his role and he had it down perfectly. He was a Financial Counselor. He would be the asshole who loved to subtly harass the uninsured and kindly remind them of how much their bill was going to be. He would offer assistance to apply for Medicaid, or Medicare if the patient appeared disabled. The Financial Counselor went above and beyond simply asking for copayments, as the Registrars did. This position was more akin to mob enforcer. If a patient tells you they can't pay, you remind them again and again that they *must* pay, and you never accept no for an answer. Jack knew of this position rather well, as it was always open, and whenever it was filled, it didn't stay that way for long. That little thing called a conscience always seemed to eat away at people.

"Can you tell me what room Anthony Miner is in?" Jack asked the clerk at the front registration office. He held a clipboard filled with empty sheets of paper to make him look more professional, but the clerk seemed completely indifferent to the world around him.

"ICU. Room 17," he said.

Room 17? Where have I heard that before?

"And where is the ICU, exactly?" Jack asked.

"East wing. Just follow the signs," the clerk said, displaying the sheer minimum of customer service possible.

"Your girl...she's here and she's not alone." Holy shit! That's where I heard Room 17. The Machete guy!

"Thank you," Jack said.

"No prob," the clerk answered.

Jack followed the long corridors of the hospital until he reached the ICU on the east side. There were 24 rooms total, and each room had to be entered through a sliding glass door. A nurse sat at her station in the middle of the room and looked at the monitors in front of her. She looked up at Jack briefly as he walked in. She would have thought nothing of him were it not for the rather large bruises that covered his face. The bruises made him stand out.

"Can I help you?" she asked him.

"I'm with Financial Counseling. I'm looking for Room 17."

"Mr. Miner? I don't think he'll be able to say anything. He certainly can't sign any consent forms right now, if that's what you're here for," the nurse said.

"No. I just have some information on applying for Medicaid that I wanted to drop off," Jack said.

"Well, sure. You can give him that. He'll need all the help he can get. Poor guy."

Poor guy? Really? Perhaps if you saw him break apart that girl's skull like an egg, you wouldn't say that.

Jack walked into Room 17 and closed the sliding door behind him. Before him was the man he had been searching for. Anthony Miner was a mess, to be sure, bruised and bloodied, much like Jack was just the previous evening. Jack wondered to himself if just pulling one simple tube or line would kill the man. He doubted it. The man was still young and healthy, his blood pressure read a very normal 117 over 76, and he seemed to be breathing quite fine on his own.

"Hello, Mr. Miner. How are we doing today?" Jack asked him and began to browse through his medical charts. The man merely shifted and grunted.

"Don't worry about it. I'll do all the talking," Jack continued and began flipping through the pages of his chart. He looked outside to see if the nurse was watching, but she seemed more concerned with her monitors than anything else in the room. When he reached the **PATIENT DEMOGRAPHICS** page, he saw something that truly surprised him. He had listed a family member as an emergency contact, and this particular family member was showing an address in Palm Grove, CA.

"So I see you lived in Palm Grove. You know, I knew some people there. Does the name Amanda Grimmits ring a bell? Or maybe her uncle…or should I say father…Dwayne Grimmits? You guys live close to each other?" he asked.

Anthony Miner opened his eyes and looked over at Jack for the first time, and his blood pressure slowly began to rise. 122/80 – 127/83 – 130/87 ….

"Uh oh? Did I say something? I have some other names for you, too. How about Max Wilkins? He was six years old. Or maybe Gabriela Johnson. Five years old. You know her, right?"

"Uhhhhhhrrrgmmmm," the man began to shout incoherently as he pressed the button for his nurse. His blood pressure now at 160 over 100. The nurse quickly ran into the room to see what was happening.

"What's going on here?" she asked Jack.

"I don't know, I just mentioned his hospital bill and he went nuts," Jack replied.

"I really wish you people would just wait for a family member and stop bothering the patients," the nurse said with a sigh.

"I'm sorry. I'll get out of your way," Jack said and left the room. He had already taken down Anthony Miner's home address, and that was his next stop.

CHAPTER 19

When Tony got the call from his friend, Dwayne, that he needed help with another body, the last thing in the world he expected was to see young Amanda Grimmits lying before him.

"What the fuck happened, man?" Tony asked his friend.

"It was an accident. A fucking accident," Dwayne told him. As they moved the body into the backyard, Tony could hear Amanda's mother, Joanne, crying hysterically in the house.

"Your niece. Your fucking niece," Tony said.

"Just shut the fuck up and help me dig. I told you it was a fucking accident. That's all there is to it."

"What about Joanne? She's okay with her girl out here? I mean…no proper burial and all?" Tony asked.

"She's fine. She'll get over it. None of us can talk about this to anyone, got it?"

"Yeah, I got it," Tony said, and continued to dig into the night.

CHAPTER 20

If any house could truly be called a *haunted* house, it was the farm house that belonged to Anthony Miner. When Jack finally arrived at the house later that evening, using the GPS on his smart phone, he immediatley felt chills all around him. He knew this house from his dream, but now that it was finally in front of him, he could truly feel the fear of every young victim that had been brought to this place. Jack thought of about a dozen different ways he could break into the house, but to his surprise, as he approached the front door, it simply *opened for him.* It was as though the house *wanted*, or *needed* him to come inside.

I just need to find something…anything…to prove his guilt. Then I can get the hell out of there.

As he stepped inside to the loud creaks of the floorboards, he could see shadows circling his feet, guiding him as to where he needed to go.

The spiral staircase. The basement. That's it, isn't it?

As Jack approached the staircase and made his way down to the basement, he could see a single flickering light. It was a light which wasn't attached to any electrical outlet. It was a light for Jack, and Jack only. He saw the table where so many of the victims had been placed, and the handcuffs. There was no blood on the table or floor, but he knew something was wrong about the room.

You haven't cleaned everything, have you? There's something here you didn't get to. You didn't expect to be sideswiped by a school bus. You thought there was plenty of time to get back here and finish the job.

Jack looked at the wall and the set of tools hanging there.

The hammer. Where is it?

When Jack finally saw the tool that had taken young Gabriela Johnson's life, it jumped out of its place on the wall and hit the ground with a loud WHACK. Had any spirits in the room been in a state of slumber, the noise surely would have awoken them. He crouched down to look at the hammer and noticed that the blood had not been completely wiped clean. Several drops had already dried into the face and neck. It was a careless mistake. One which Mr. Miner surely would have caught himself were he not lying in an ICU bed at St. Paul's North Austin Medical Center.

This is it. This is enough to get the police in here. One anonymous call and this guy is fucked.

As much as Jack wanted to kill the man himself, and how he *did* want that, he knew the risk far outweighed the reward. He knew Texas, with its very rich history of capital punishment, would execute this man as fast as the courts would possibly allow. Justice, he reasoned, would still prevail in the long run. He thought about what he would say when he called 911. He knew the police were desperate for any leads on this case, and would pounce on whatever he gave them.

As Jack made his way out of the house, he noticed a police cruiser heading his way, its blue and red lights flashing without a siren.

Ah shit! I'd better come up with a story about what I'm doing here pretty quick.

The cruiser pulled up next to Jack's car, and a rather large, burly man stepped out and looked at Jack.

"Howdy!" the policeman said.

"Good evening," Jack replied.

"My name is Sheriff Tom Jackson. I'm with Elgin PD. You know this area is all private property, don't ya? You visiting someone around here? You a friend of Tony Miner?" the Sheriff asked.

"No…umm…actually, I was planning on moving out here. Relocating. I just wanted to get a feel for the area," Jack said.

"At night? Don't take me for a fool, son. Ain't nothin' but farm folk out here. Now I notice by your license plate that you're from California, and you don't look like no farmer to me. You lost or something?" the Sheriff asked him.

"Yeah. Actually, I was just driving around Austin. I took a few wrong turns and I ended up out here somehow," Jack explained.

Oh, God. My answers are getting worse by the minute.

"Austin? That's about 40 minutes west of here. You're in Elgin. Your little electronic doo dad phone should have told you that."

"Well, I wasn't using the GPS, and I kinda lost track of time," Jack said.

"Son…now I been a sheriff for a long time. Really long. I've heard about every lie you can think of. People will say just about anything to get themselves out of trouble. And I just ain't buyin' what you're sellin' me. So, if you don't want me to haul you in to the station for trespassing, you better start telling me the truth," Sheriff Jackson told him.

"Not sure you'll believe the truth, either," Jack said.

"Try me, son."

"That house," Jack said, pointing. "The man who lives there is a serial killer. He's killed at least half a dozen kids in that house. Maybe more. All you have to do is go in there and you'll find the evidence you need to lock him up."

"What are ya, some kind of psychic?" Sheriff Jackson asked him, scratching his head. "We don't just lock people up based on some outer-space mumbo jumbo."

"Just go in there. You'll see," Jack said.

"I just can't walk into someone's house without reasonable suspicion. Now, if you saw something in there that you believe was suspicious activity, that's a whole 'nother matter. But I can't just walk in for no reason," the Sheriff explained.

"How about a bloody murder weapon. Is that good enough?" Jack asked him.

"You *saw* that? How the hell could you have seen that from the outside?"

"I didn't," Jack said. "I was inside."

"Breaking and entering! Jesus jumpin' Christ! Do you realize what kind of trouble you're in, boy?" the Sheriff said.

"Please…just go in there," Jack pleaded.

"Okay. I'll play along with you because I'm a nice guy. But if I don't see what you think is in there, you're coming out of here in handcuffs."

"Fine," Jack said.

"You first. Lead the way."

· · · · ·

Jack led the sheriff down the staircase into the basement.

"Be careful, there's no light down here and I couldn't find the sw…" Jack began.

"I think I found it," Sheriff Jackson said, flipping the switch on a side panel in the wall. The room lit up quite brightly.

"There!" Jack said, pointing at the hammer on the floor. "That's it. That's the weapon he used to kill Gabriela Johnson."

"Let me see that," the Sheriff said to Jack. "Hand it to me, please."

As Jack bent down to pick up the hammer, he could hear the Sheriff's revolver being drawn from its holster. As he swung around he heard the click of the hammer, and then the shot. The pain was sharp and quick, and blood began to pour from his stomach.

"Gut wound," Sheriff Jackson said. "You won't die right away. Might take a few hours."

Jack held his stomach and fell back onto the hard, concrete floor. The blood began to flow between the cracks in his fingers. "Why?" he asked.

"You think I'm gonna let someone like you, a piece of trash from California, take down my little brother?" Sheriff Jackson told him. "I don't give a shit if you had psychic visions, or the fuckin' Virgin Mary, or even God Almighty sent you here. You're somewhere you ain't supposed to be."

"You're the one he talked to on the phone that night. It was you. It's always been the two of you," Jack whispered.

"You seem to know a whole hell of a lot, don't ya? Now listen up. We can either get this done quick, or we can take our time. What I want to know is, are you here with anyone else, and who have you told this story to? Answer those two questions for me and I promise I'll make it quick and painless. Your other option is to simply bleed out, and trust me, you don't want that. That's a lot of agonizing pain."

"Fuck you," Jack said. "Fucking child killer."

The sheriff walked over to Jack, kicking him in the stomach. He then removed Jack's wallet and began to rifle through it. A fairly recent picture of Jack and Jennifer caught his eye very quickly.

"Well, well, well. What do we have here? Your daughter?" he asked.

"You heard me. Go FUCK yourself," Jack shouted.

"You ain't gotta tell me. It's pretty God damn obvious. You got quite a few pictures of her in your wallet. Now, you don't strike me as someone who's into teenage pussy, so I have to assume this is your daughter. Do I assume correct?" the Sheriff asked him tauntingly.

"If you fucking touch her…" Jack began.

"What? I love it when someone is dying and they try to suddenly act brave. What are you going to do? You're going to kill me? Is that it? Just how are you going to do that, Mr. Jack Taylor?" he asked, reading Jack's name from the driver's license.

"You didn't let me finish my sentence," Jack said. "I was going to say…if you fucking touch her, I'm not the one you'll have to worry about."

"Really. You got me quaking in my boots over a teenage girl, Jack. Now..what's this?" he asked, pulling out a receipt from Jack's back pocket. "Extended Stay on Research Boulevard. I guess this is where you're staying. So, if I happen to go there, will I find that hot little piece of tail that's your daughter there, too?"

"She's not there. I'm alone," Jack said.

"Well, I can't say you're very trustworthy, Mr. Taylor. I think I'll go down there and see what I can find. In the meantime…" Sheriff Jackson began and grabbed Jack's hands, putting them behind his back and handcuffing him to a drain pipe on the wall. "I need to make sure you stay put. If I find your daughter, I'll bring her back here and we can have a little family reunion. So don't die on me. Not yet."

CHAPTER 21

Jennifer knew something had gone wrong when the voice at the hotel room door was not her father's. When she heard the knock, she assumed that he had simply misplaced his key, but when Sheriff Tom Jackson spoke, she knew something bad must have happened.

"Miss Taylor? You in there? This is Sheriff Tom Jackson of Elgin PD. I need to ask you a few questions. It's about your father," he said through the door.

Jennifer walked to the door and cracked it open, still leaving the chain on.

"Can I see your badge?" she asked him.

"Absolutely, ma'am," he replied politely. He pulled out the badge and held it in front of him. "Satisfied?" he asked.

"Where is my father?" Jennifer asked.

"Well, he's asked me to come and get you. It seems he had a car accident. He's fine and all, don't worry about that. He's more embarassed than hurt, actually. He just wanted me to come and pick you up," the Sheriff told her.

"Why doesn't he just call me himself?" Jennifer asked suspiciously.

"Seems his cell phone was damaged. He couldn't get a hold of you," the Sheriff replied.

"It doesn't really make sense that the police Sheriff would go to so much trouble for a simple traffic accident," Jennifer said.

"You always been this distrustful of law enforcement, ma'am?"

"Don't call me, ma'am," Jennifer said.

"Sorry. Miss Taylor. And if you really want to know, Elgin PD goes above and beyond for all its residents, and to visitors just passing through. Now can you please open the door so we can talk?"

"Sure, but just to be safe, I think I'll call the Elgin PD just to confirm my dad is okay, and to make sure he's got enough help," Jennifer said.

"That's completely unnecessary. We've got it all taken care of," the Sheriff said.

"Then I guess they'll tell me that when I call them," Jennifer said and walked over to the hotel room phone. As she began to dial, the Sheriff burst through the door with all his weight.

"You little bitch!" he shouted and grabbed her by the arm.

"Get the fuck off me! I'm not going anywhere with you!" Jennifer shouted back, but the Sheriff was too powerful. He had already prepared a small towel filled with chloroform, which he kept behind his back while they were talking. He pressed it against her face, and within seconds she was out.

• • • • •

Jennifer awoke to find herself lying on the table in the basement of the old farm house. Her hands and ankles were both handcuffed to the legs of the table.

"What the fuck is going on?!" she shouted, and then she saw her father in the corner. His face had gone pale. If he wasn't dead yet, she figured, he didn't have much time left. "Dad!"

"Well, you're finally awake," the Sheriff said. "Daddy boy over there...well...he doesn't look so good."

"You mother fucker!" Jennifer shouted.

"Jesus, girl! You're just a little kid and you already have a mouth like that?"

"Go fuck yourself, asshole! You're just a fucking pedophile piece-of-shit cop who gets his kicks murdering little kids!"

"Jen…" Jack said from the back of the room.

"Hey, he's still alive!" the Sheriff said and smiled.

"Dad! Are you okay?" Jennifer shouted.

"Remember what I said to you about your…gift? About how you needed to control it and hide it away?" Jack said.

"Yes," Jennifer replied, crying. "I remember."

"Forget that. Use it. Kill this fucker and get out of here," he said.

The Sheriff then walked over to Jack, pointed his revolver at his head, and pulled the trigger.

"No!" Jennifer screamed hysterically. The Sheriff then turned to Jennifer.

"Your turn, girl. Sorry about this. It ain't personal," he said and raised his revolver at her.

A rush of light began to fill the room as Jennifer's face began to turn a bright pink. She could see Amanda standing behind the Sheriff, watching with delight. Max was there, too, and Gabriela, and all the other kids who had died in this terrible place.

The revolver began to fall apart in the Sheriff's hand like it was being crushed in a vise. He could then begin to feel all the bones in his hand begin to break, and he let out a scream much like that of his victims. Jennifer then set her sights on her handcuffs, which all snapped off as if it were some simple magic trick.

"You fucking bitch!" the Sheriff screamed.

"Doesn't feel good, does it?" Jennifer asked him.

She looked at his legs, and with a simple stare, they both cracked like toothpicks, sending the Sheriff crashing to the floor. He fell into a position that almost resembled an awkward dance move, with each mangled leg facing a separate direction.

"What the fuck are you?" the Sheriff shouted at her through his unbearable pain.

"I'm the one who is about to end your miserable fucking existence. And when I'm done with you, I'm going to see your brother. And he'll die in just as much pain as you are in now," she said.

"Fuck you!" the Sheriff shouted. He began to feel an intense weight coming down on his head. Jennifer had directed her sights on his skull.

"I'd say it's not personal. But it is," Jennifer said as the Sheriff's skull began to break apart from the inside. His face collapsed upon itself, sending a river of blood pouring through his eyes and nose. Then she worked on the rest of his body, and when she had finished, he looked as though he had been run over by a steamroller, and then run over a second and third time.

CHAPTER 22

"Dwanye is dead!" Tony shouted over the phone to his big brother, Tommy.

"Calm down, little brother. Tell me what happened?" Tommy asked.

"It was Joanne. She killed him. Blew his fucking head off. The cops are all over their backyard now. They're finding all the bodies!" Tony shouted.

"Relax. Has your name even been mentioned?" Tommy asked.

"I don't know. I don't think so. It looks like they're just lookin' at Dwayne right now. But it ain't good."

"All right, listen. What you need to do is get out of Palm Grove. That's a shit town, anyway. Come out here to Texas. I'll help you get set up someplace. But don't make it look obvious. Wait until the morning. Don't make it look like you're trying to run," Tommy said.

"Okay, I won't," Tony said.

"Jesus, man. What were you guys up to out there?"

"You know, man. The usual. Just havin' some fun," Tony replied.

"Having fun, huh? You were always the weird one, Tony. Maybe if we had the same father, you wouldn't have been so fucked up," Tommy said.

"Sorry I couldn't become the big shot deputy you are."

"Just get your ass out here and don't look back."

CHAPTER 23

When Anthony Miner awoke in his hospital bed, the last thing he expected to see was a thirteen-year-old standing by his bedside. Though he didn't know who she was, her presence pleased him, and he gave her a smile.

"You my nurse?" he whispered. He was still weak, and his voice had not returned to him completely.

"Yes, I am," Jennifer replied as she pushed the first syringe into his stomach.

"Nurses are getting' cuter every day," he told her.

"Ah, you're just sayin' that," Jennifer replied as she took out a second syringe and injected him once again into his stomach.

"Ow!" Anthony whispered loudly. "That kinda hurts. I can feel it burning. What was that?"

"That was about 64 ccs of bleach that I've just injected directly into your body. It'll start eating through your internal organs in a few minutes, causing massive bleeding. You'll experience the worst pain you've ever had in your life, and then you'll die," Jennifer explained.

"What?" he asked her, hoping it was a joke, but he knew it wasn't. He could feel the chemicals in his body eating away at him.

"Have a nice day," Jennifer said and quickly left his room.

. . . . .

As Jennifer left the hospital, she could hear the alarms going off from inside. She knew she would end up on some surveillance video somewhere, but she didn't care. As she walked into the parking lot, a large black van pulled up beside her. A man in a black suit and sunglasses got out and looked at her.

"Jennifer Taylor. Please get into the van," he said.

"I'm not going with you," she said.

"Please. It's either this or the cops. And you don't want the cops to get you. Trust me," the man said.

Jennifer could see Mr. Phillips as she stepped up into the van.

"Hello, Jennifer," Mr. Phillips said to her. "Seems you've been busy."

"I don't know what you're talking about," Jennifer replied.

"Well, we've got a local Sheriff that's a human pancake, and God only knows what you just did to poor ol' Mr. Miner in there," Mr. Phillips said.

"They deserved it. They were murderers. They killed my dad," Jennifer told him.

"Of course they deserved it. You absolutely did the right thing. Those men were the scum of the earth. Good riddance, I say. But, there will be those who will want to bring you down, too. Cops don't care too much for vigilante justice," Mr. Phillips explained.

"I don't care."

"Then come with me. No one can touch you where I'll take you. You'll be perfectly safe. You'll finish your education. You'll have a nice place to live and everything you can possibly want will be right at your fingertips. And then later on…we can talk about you working for us. Helping your country,"

"And if I say no?" Jennifer asked.

"Then you'll be on your own. You'll face charges for the Sheriff and his brother. Now, granted, you're just a minor, and it won't be particularly harsh. Especially when word gets out that these two gentleman were psychotic pieces of shit. But still, you'll spend some time in a youth prison. You probably won't like that that, Jennifer."

"Fine. I'll go with you. But don't call me Jennifer anymore," she said.

"Sure. What shall I call you?" he asked.

"My name is Amanda."

ABOUT THE AUTHOR

Ken Berglund was born and raised in Southern California, spending most of his early years in Downey and Long Beach. He spent 4 1/2 years in Asia working as an English teacher in Taiwan. He met his wife Chien Yu (Christy) while working for Hess Language School in Hsinchu. His experiences in Taiwan were documented in his first book, "An American Teacher in Taiwan." He has two children.

Ken moved his family to Austin, Texas in 2008, and his struggles and successes were documented in his second book, "From Taiwan to Texas: Life in Mid-America." His third book, "The Reluctant Austinite," is the third and final book in a trilogy of memoirs & anecdotes about life in America and Taiwan. His first fiction book, "Interstate 10", was released in January of 2013 to very positive reviews. He followed up that book with another fiction book, "Small Town Evil", in February 2013. "Small Town Evil" became a massive hit. It quickly entered the Amazon Top 50 Best Seller List (reaching a high of #3) and stayed on there for well over a year, selling tens of thousands of copies, and at one point only being outsold by veteran horror writers Stephen King and Anne Rice. "I still can't believe it," Ken said about the success of STE. "You always hope your book will sell well, though often it doesn't. With my previous books, if I sold ten copies in a month, I would consider that something. I would brag to my wife 'Hey, ten copies this month!' and she'd be impressed. Then 'Small Town Evil' comes out and I'm selling 100 copies in a single day, and not just for one or two days, but for months on end. It's unreal. I really don't know what it was about that book that struck a nerve with people."

His next book, "The Dead Ones" was released in April of 2013. Ken described "The Dead Ones" as "Sort of a companion piece to 'Interstate 10.' If you liked 'Interstate 10', you would probably like this one as well."

"Four Bites", a compilation of stories both old and new, was released in November, 2013

"Small Town Evil 2", the much anticipated sequel to Ken's biggest seller, was released in March of 2014. "I wasn't really sure I wanted to write a sequel," Ken said. "But the response to that book was so overwhelming. Those who loved the book wanted a sequel, and those who didn't like it complained that it lacked closure. I know I can't please everyone, but maybe this second book will give them the closure they are looking for."

OTHER BOOKS BY KEN BERGLUND

FICTION

SMALL TOWN EVIL

INTERSTATE 10

THE DEAD ONES

FOUR BITES

NON-FICTION

AN AMERICAN TEACHER IN TAIWAN

FROM TAIWAN TO TEXAS: LIFE IN MID-AMERICA

THE RELUCTANT AUSTINITE

Author Page: http://www.amazon.com/Ken-Berglund/e/B00AQ53N2Q/ref=sr_tc_2_0?qid=139353836 6&sr=8-2-ent

Facebook Page:
https://www.facebook.com/kenberglundwriter

www.ingramcontent.com/pod-product-compliance
Lightning Source LLC
LaVergne TN
LVHW011253200326
834410LV00006B/240